REPORT CARD

GRADING PERIOD	1	2	3	4
FUNDAMENTALS OF ART 1	A-	A	A	A-
EARTH SCIENCE	B+	B	B+	B-
ENGLISH 1	A	A	A	A-
INTRO TO MUSIC	C	C+	B-	C-
MATH SKILLS 1	A-	B+	A-	B
PHYSICAL EDUCATION	A	A	A	A-
SPANISH	B+	B+	B+	B+
Grade Average	B+	B+	B+	B
Attendance: Present	40	40	38	40
Absent	0	0	2	0
Tardy	0	0	0	0

A = Excellent B = Good C = Satisfactory N= Needs Improvement
U = Unsatisfactory I = Insufficient/Incomplete

Student: Julie Graham-Chang   Grade: B+   Year: 6

I got all A's in Art!

I'm not surprised.

I'm going to rock the Youth Arts Workshop this summer.
Have you asked your dads if you could do it yet?

5

They've been really busy lately.

WHAT TO DO THIS SUMMER
LYDIA EDITION
MARTIAL ARTS CAMP!

Pros I will get awesomer at martial arts. I may even go so far as to become a Martial Arts Master.
~~Also~~
Chuck will be there!

CONS I might get too awesome at martial arts, so awesome that it would be wrong not to become some sort of secret crime-fighter and I don't know if I'm ready for that sort of responsibility.

I don't know if the world is ready for you to take on that sort of responsibility.

Also, Chuck will be there, and he's still mad because he thinks I tried to break him and Jane up.

jladybugaboo: Are you online? Are you online?

goldstandard3000: Are you online???

jladybugaboo: Yes!

goldstandard3000: YES CAN YOU BELIEVE IT?

jladybugaboo: What do you think it's going to be about?

goldstandard3000: Well, you remember what happened the last time they called a Double Family Meeting!

THREE YEARS AGO...

We, your fantastic parents, have called this Double Family Meeting to tell you...

We're going on vacation together!

Three years ago our parents got together and surprised us with a trip to the shore. It was really fun. For everyone who wasn't trying to stay as pale as humanly possible.

POSSIBLE VACATION SPOTS!

HAWAII?

NEW YORK CITY?

MT. EVEREST?

THE MOON?

The Moon? Really?
I got an A in Art! That means I get to draw what I want.

Well, that was unexpected!

How long will we be gone?
Why are Nana and Grandpa Jim moving?
How will we get to California?
Will we be stopping anywhere else?
Will there be internet access?
Can we visit Sukie in San Francisco?
What are we going to do with Melody?

Then Daddy and Papa Dad explained that we'll fly out to San Francisco and help my grandparents move, and then drive back across the country with a bunch of Nana and Grandpa Jim's stuff in a trailer. The whole trip will take a month!! Also we're going to visit a bunch of people on our way back home.

And Melody is going to be in <u>Guatemala</u>. She's volunteering for Habitat for Humanity. In <u>Guatemala</u>.

Guatemala!

Melody in traditional Guatemalan dress!

15

From: jladybugaboo
To: sukiejaithoms100

Hi Sukie,

Guess what? We're coming to San Francisco! My dads need to help my grandparents move. I know that you're visiting your cousins in San Francisco for the summer and I was hoping that we could hang out. Lydia's coming, too, MAYBE (she has to decide if she wants to come with us or go with her mom to London for the summer).

Are you going to be around?
PLEASEPLEASEPLEASEPLEASEPLEASE SAY YES!

Love,
Julie

From: sukiejaithoms100
To: jladybugaboo

YES! YES! YES! YES!!!!!!!!!!!!!
YESYESYESYESYESYESYES!!! So, so excited, I've been here for two weeks now and I can totally show you guys around the city and my cousin took me to the BEST burrito place and we can totally go there. YAY!!!

When will you know if Lydia's coming? Tell her she has to come!

DECISION TIME

It's really weird — I want to go with Julie and the Graham-Changs, but I don't want my mom to feel like I'm abandoning her. I have to talk with her.

goldstandard3000: Just finished talking to my mom.

jladybugaboo: So? Are you coming with us?

goldstandard3000: She told me something kind of weird.

jladybugaboo: ???

goldstandard3000: She said that if I went with you guys, we could stop off at Pueblo on the way home to see my dad.

jladybugaboo: Oh. That's neat. Right?

goldstandard3000: Yeah, I guess so.

jladybugaboo: So that means you're coming?

My dad lives in Pueblo, Colorado, with my stepmother, Brenna, and her two kids. The last time that Melody and I went to see my dad (about two years ago) things didn't go so well. But he still sends presents on my birthday and calls me.

Dad

Brenna

Brenna's kids

Kyle   Cody

Melody's made it pretty clear that she never wants to talk to Dad again, but that doesn't mean I can't. I think my mom wants me to go.

It would be good to spend a little time with your dad, he really misses you.

goldstandard3000: I'M IN!!!

We all leave in a WEEK!

The packing has begun!

goldstandard3000: Are you bringing a jacket?

jladybugaboo: No, just a hoodie. We're going to San Francisco, how cold can it be?

Even Roland is leaving for the summer to visit his family in Norway.

We're going to visit mine besteforeldre in Bergen and then we're all going to stay in a hytter and eat sildebrikke and fiskeboller! I cannot wait.

I'm sure what you just said makes total sense to you.

Let's trade addresses so we can send postcards!

I told him that we were going to be on the road most of the time but he insisted, so I gave him the addresses of some of the places we'll be going.

We leave for California **TOMORROW!**
Melody left yesterday. It was weird to say goodbye to her.

Papa Dad and Daddy invited their friends' daughter, Sue, to live in our house and take care of Bad Cat while we're away.

Who's a sweet kitty? Are you a sweetie-sweetest sweet kitty?

She seems... less than smart.
Did you tell her to keep her bedroom door locked at night?
I think she thought we were joking.

We are EN ROUTE

Julie already got in trouble with the flight attendant for drawing on the emergency safety instructions. I thought they were ours to keep!

Map of our
AWESOME CROSS

San Francisco, CA

Pueblo, CO
Mr. Goldblatt
(Lydia's Dad)

Nana and Grandpa Jim
(Papa Dad's Parents)

I wonder what people are like in California.

What do you mean?

In London there were all these different rules for being popular— I wonder if it's different in other parts of the United States?

We will observe! And we will record!

Do we have to wear pith helmets?

I guess not.

After the long flight Nana and Grandpa Jim picked us up from the airport in San Francisco. It was great to see them but I think Grandpa Jim believes I'm still five years old.

Yikes!

How's my little Julie-bear?

I think your Grandpa Jim believes your dads are still five years old.

How are my boys? My boys are looking good!

Hi Dad.

Grandpa Jim is crazy strong.

When we got to Nana and Grandpa Jim's house, most of their stuff had already been packed up, but there was a whole pile of stuff that we're supposed to take back home with us.

Here are some boxes for your Aunt Kat, and some things I've saved for you!

Julie, you get my macramé owl! You used to stare at it for hours when you were little!

I used to stare at it for hours because I was afraid that if I looked away it would kill me and eat me. It's terrifying. Maybe we can set it free when we're driving through the Rocky Mountains. Owls like mountains, right?

Because everything in my grandparents' house is in boxes, we're staying in a hotel until the move is finished.

There's a map of the hotel in our room, with evacuation instructions in the event of **AN EARTHQUAKE.**

OUR PLAN IN THE EVENT OF AN EARTHQUAKE

1. Scream.
2. Hide under the bed.
3. Scream some more.
4. Cry.
5. Quickly come up with last words that are deep and meaningful.

Tomorrow, while Daddy and Papa Dad help with the move, we're going to hang out in San Francisco with Sukie!

If we survive the night...

We survived the night!
It was really good to see Sukie. She seemed a lot happier than the last time we saw her.
That was at her mom's funeral.
True. But still, she seemed pretty great. We met up with Sukie and her cousin at the Japanese Tea Garden in Golden Gate Park, which was so, so pretty.

Do you miss your mom?

I do, a lot, but she was sick for most of my life. It's been months since I've been in a hospital and I don't miss that.

Afterward Sukie's cousin took us to the Mission District to get burritos. It seemed like a long way to go to get a burrito.

BUT THEY WERE THE BEST BURRITOS. We stood in line for a half hour to get the burritos, and they were still **THE BEST BURRITOS**. EVER. I'm spoiled for burritos. For life. I'll never again eat a burrito as good as the burrito I ate today. EVER. It's only been a few hours and I already miss them.

After the burritos we all went to Fisherman's Wharf.
And had to drive up and down the craziest, steepest, scariest hills to get there.

I was pretty sure we were going to slide into the car behind us and keep sliding and crashing until we reached the San Francisco Bay.

SO SCARY. But Fisherman's Wharf was great. We watched piles and piles of seals loafing around the docks. They were so cute! And also stinky.

Just like you!

HEY!

After we had dinner Sukie's cousin drove us back to the hotel. Daddy and Papa Dad had spent the day moving and unpacking stuff at Nana and Grandpa Jim's new house, and I don't think they were in a talking sort of mood.

In the morning we drove down to Nana and Grandpa Jim's new house in Half Moon Bay. It's a lot smaller than their old house, but it's a five-minute walk from the Pacific Ocean and also really close to an ice cream shop. We spent most of the day unpacking stuff. Your grandparents own an enormous hugantic ridiculous amount of books. Daddy definitely thinks so.

Let me know if you see any you want. You can take them home with you!

Don't you dare. I'm never ever lifting a book again.

BOOKS L.R.   BOOKS L.R.   BOOK

When we were too tired to unpack anything else, we ran out to the beach. Which was ~~freezing~~. Why is California so cold? Isn't it supposed to be warm in the summer? You promised it would be warm!
I don't know what you're talking about. We emailed about it! And printed the email and pasted it in this book! You told me not to bring a jacket!

So... this is nice.

I can't feel my feet.

But it was really pretty. True.

WE ARE ON THE ROAD!

The Dads rented this big car with a trailer that's full of Nana and Grandpa Jim's old stuff.

That owl is in there somewhere. I think I can feel it watching me.

Daddy and Papa Dad are insisting that one goal of our trip is to learn all the words to the song "American Pie."

It's like a half hour long! Unfair.

And it's not even about pie. Unfair.

First Stop: FRESNO, CALIFORNIA

Fresno is about 3½ hours away from Half Moon Bay.

Fresno is the fifth-largest city in California, and home to the first modern landfill in the United States.

Exciting! Fresno is also home to the Forestiére Underground Gardens, which we're going to visit when we're done with lunch.

Papa Dad is insisting we write down that Fresno is also the Birthplace of Denim Jeans, and we're all fools for ignoring that and choosing to see awesome underground gardens instead.

OUTVOTED!

We're in the Forestiere Underground Gardens!
So neat. Why don't we have an
underground garden?

The Gardens were made by this guy.
Baldasare Forestiere, over 40 years. He
didn't like being above ground where it was
too hot, So he dug these caves to live
in and planted trees in them.
It's much cooler in here

WE SURVIVED AN EARTHQUAKE!!!

I can't believe we're still alive. We were looking at Baldasare Forestiere's living quarters and Papa Dad was trying to convince Julie that if she had been a boy she would have been named "Baldasare," and then the **GROUND STARTED SHAKING** and we all ran out of the cave.

It was so scary. The earthquake only lasted a few seconds and was pretty much over by the time we got above ground. Then Julie threw up. It was horrible.

We decided to just jump in the car and drive as far east as we could go. After a few hours we ended up here, in a motel in Yermo, California.

Home sweet motel

Papa Dad went out to look for food for us while Lydia, Daddy, and I watched the television for news of the earthquake.
They're calling it a "minor" earthquake!!
WE ALMOST DIED!!!
Papa Dad is back. I'm pretty sure he bought our dinner at a 24-hour convenience store.

Breakfast! It's nice to be eating real food again.

You'd think eating chips and peanut butter sandwiches for dinner would be kind of fun, but you'd be wrong.

Fun Fact about Yermo! There hasn't been an earthquake here today!

YAY!!

Also, we're next to a ghost town.

So we're going to Calico now, which is a genuine Old West ghost town named after a genuine Old West dead cat.

Cowcat Ghost

mrowooooo

EVERYTHING HERE IS GENUINE OLD WEST!

GENUINE OLD WEST SODA!

GENUINE OLD WEST GEAR!

GENUINE OLD WEST REFRIGERATOR MAGNETS!

GENUINE OLD WEST SNOWGLOBES!

GENUINE OLD WEST CHICKEN FINGERS AT THE GENUINE OLD WEST CAFÉ!

I think Papa Dad could use some Genuine Old West Sunblock.

After Daddy took a million billion pictures and we bought some Genuine Old West postcards, we got back in the car and drove for five hours to get to Flagstaff, Arizona.

About two of those hours were spent arguing over what to name the rental car.

Let's name it Hrimfaxi!

Hrum-whah?

It's the name of a Norse god's horse.

Let's name it Roland!

No.

That's ridiculous.

How about Katana?

How about Bob?

Let's name it Giles.

This is how Bad Cat got her name.

What it's like to drive through
ARIZONA
Sedimentary Rocks
Spooky Hills
No one else for miles around

The other 3½ hours were spent listening to Fun Facts about Arizona.

The capital of Arizona is Phoenix. The highest elevation in Arizona, at 12,633 ft, is Humphreys Peak, and 1.54% of the population speaks Navajo! The extra great thing is that I've gathered Fun Facts on every state that we'll be driving through, so no one has to worry about being uninformed.

Can you read those while driving?

No.

Good. I'm pulling over. You're taking the wheel.

Also, Daddy had to stop every single time we saw a gas station because he was afraid we would run out of gas in the middle of the desert.

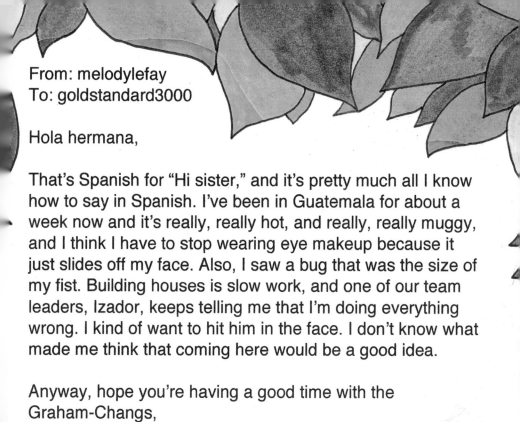

From: melodylefay
To: goldstandard3000

Hola hermana,

That's Spanish for "Hi sister," and it's pretty much all I know how to say in Spanish. I've been in Guatemala for about a week now and it's really, really hot, and really, really muggy, and I think I have to stop wearing eye makeup because it just slides off my face. Also, I saw a bug that was the size of my fist. Building houses is slow work, and one of our team leaders, Izador, keeps telling me that I'm doing everything wrong. I kind of want to hit him in the face. I don't know what made me think that coming here would be a good idea.

Anyway, hope you're having a good time with the Graham-Changs,
Melody

From: goldstandard3000
To: melodylefay

Hi Mel!

We're in a hotel in Flagstaff. So far we've survived an EARTHQUAKE and a RATTLESNAKE ATTACK. Okay, the rattlesnake attack didn't actually happen, but we saw a rattlesnake on the side of the road. It was probably a rattlesnake. It might have been a part of a blown-out tire, but still, we survived an EARTHQUAKE.

Hope things go better for you soon. Maybe you can find one of those bugs and put it in Izador's bed or something.

Love,
Hermana Lydia

Someone had the brilliant idea to leave Flagstaff at DAWN so that we could spend more time in New Mexico, so here we are on the road again.

I liked Flagstaff. I was sleeping in Flagstaff. Now I'm not sleeping anymore. I like this much less.

One nickname for New Mexico is "The Land of Enchantment," and the state's motto is "Crescit Eundo," which means "It grows as it goes." The capital of New Mexico is our destination, Albuquerque. Fun Fact! I know a song called "Point Me in the Direction of Albuquerque." Anyone want to hear me sing it?

NO.

After all of Papa Dad's Fun Facts,
Daddy asked me how I felt about
seeing my dad again. I didn't really
have an answer ~~because~~ I don't
know how I feel.

When my parents divorced, my dad
married Brenna and moved away
to Pueblo. It kind of sucked
because even though Dad called every
week, we never got to see him,
but then Melody and I went to
visit him. It was not a good trip.

I can't say that Melody was being pleasant, but she's Melody — she's never pleasant. Kyle and Cody would not stop making fun of her.

Are you a vampire?

Ha Ha Ha, Vampire Girl!

Shut up, you little jerks.

Dad really didn't know what to do with her.

As long as you're in my house you will treat your brothers with respect, young lady. It's bad enough that your mother lets you dress like a freak, but I will not have you picking on the boys.

Brenna was trying to be nice,
I guess. but she mostly just
paid attention to me. She had
bought all these clothes for me
and insisted on doing my hair
and makeup.

You are going to be the prettiest princess in the whole pageant!

what are you doing to her?

When Melody saw what Brenna
was doing, she **EXPLODED.**

My sister is Not your DOLL!!!

Then things got really bad. My dad heard Melody shouting at Brenna, then he shouted at Melody, and everyone was shouting, and Melody shut herself up in a room and called our mom, and the next thing I knew she was packing our bags and we were getting in a cab to go to the airport. We had to wait forever until we could get a flight home.

Melody hasn't spoken with Dad since. He still calls me sometimes.

We are now in ALBUQUERQUE!!

Fun Fact! Every year Albuquerque has an enormous Balloon Fiesta. Lame Fact - we're not here at the right time to go to the Balloon Fiesta. Papa Dad believes that because Balloon Fiesta postcards are everywhere in Albuquerque, it's like we were at the Fiesta. I believe Papa Dad has had a little too much sun.

The dads tried to make us see the sights of Albuquerque but after we discovered that the hotel had a pool, we kind of rejected that idea.

We couldn't hear them! We were underwater!

Who wants to see a historic hacienda?

Tonight we're going out to see a minor league baseball game.

The ALBUQUERQUE ISOTOPES vs. the FRESNO GRIZZLIES

MATCHUP of the MILLENNIUM!

Since we don't know anything about the teams, we don't know who to root for. But we won't let that stop us!

LYDIA and PAPA DAD vs. JULIE and DADDY

MATCHUP of the MINUTE!

Parker, the Grizzlies Mascot

Some sort of alien dog

Orbit, the Isotopes Mascot

A grizzly bear could easily take down an alien dog. Go Grizzlies! Let's not make the home team fans mad at us! Go Isotopes!

We decided that the fans of the losing team had to buy dinner for the fans of the winning team, so Papa Dad and Lydia had to buy us hot dogs.

Which I suspect we would have bought for dinner anyway.

Go Isotopes!

Before we drive to Pueblo we're going to go to the Rattlesnake Museum in Albuquerque. Daddy says it's educational, but we think he just wants to prove that what he saw on the side of the road in Arizona was really a rattlesnake and we were actually in terrible danger.

Fun Facts about RATTLESNAKES!

- Their fangs are retractable!
- Their venom breaks down blood and/or paralyzes nerves!
- A new segment is added to their rattles every time they shed their skin!
- They are ovoviviparous, which means they give birth to live babies! (Instead of eggs.)
- A large majority of rattle snakes live in the American Southwest, which is where we are right now!

It kinda does look like a torn-up tire.

That's nice of you to say, sweetie.

On the road to **PUEBLO.**

We're going to spend the first night in Pueblo with Mr. Goldblatt and his family. and then Daddy, Papa Dad, and I are going to head north to Denver to visit their old college buddies for a few days so that Lydia can spend Quality Time with her dad.

Then you're all coming back to pick me up when Quality Time is over.

Are you nervous about seeing your dad?

He's my dad. What's there to be nervous about?

Who wants to hear some Fun Facts about Pueblo?

When we got out of the car
Brenna came running up to us
and immediately hugged Lydia.

It was weird to see Lydia's dad again.

After we unloaded
Hrimfaxi ~~Katana~~
Daddy did a load of
laundry in the
Goldblatts' washing
machine. Daddy
was so happy.

~~Were we smelly?~~ I didn't think so,
but now I'm not sure...after we put the
clothes in the dryer we went out for dinner.

This place has the BEST burritos!

Mr. Goldblatt's family seems okay, just like they're trying a little too hard. Especially Brenna.

I don't think that Kyle or Cody are trying too hard. Or trying anything at all.

SEPARATION CHECKLIST

JULIE	LYDIA

Trip notebook
○————————○

Colored pencils
○————————○

Some markers, because Lydia can't possibly need all the markers
○————————○

Some pages from the trip notebook, for note-taking
○————————●

Markers, but not all of them, because Julie will go bonkers without her art supplies
●————————●

I will not.
Sure you won't.

I don't have the right shade of blue. I will surely perish!

I'm not this bad. Sure you aren't.

After Julie and Dad and Papa Dad left for Denver I went with my dad and his family to Lake Pueblo State Park to go whitewater rafting. I was excited even though Kyle and Cody said that the park was stupid.

> Do we have to go?

> We're really busy.

OBSERVATION: Kyle and Cody are never really busy.

But I was having a good time in the boat. At first.

It wasn't very rapid-y (our raft leader, Val, told us that there hasn't been a whole lot of rain this year) but it was still nice to be on the water. Even Kyle and Cody seemed to be having a nice time, until they tried to scare me.

I bet she doesn't know how to swim.

I know how to swim.

Ha ha, girls can't swim!

I bet if I threw you overboard, you'd sink.

I bet if I threw you overboard, you'd cry like a baby.

Yeah, right, like you could throw me overboard.

So I threw him overboard.

First of all, the water wasn't deep. I COULD STAND IN IT.

EVIDENCE:

me, not even close to drowning

Second, Kyle is a HUGE BABY.

Lydia threw me in! Lydia wants me to drown to death!

I saw her do it! Lydia tried to kill Kyle!

Kyle refused to get back in the boat so we all had to walk on shore back to the parking lot while Val took the boat down the river. Then Brenna said to me

Don't worry, honey, I know you didn't mean to push Kyle. Accidents happen!

goldstandard3000: It wasn't an accident! Kyle was just being a big baby because I did to him what he had been trying to do to me. We didn't even get to go over any good rapids.

jladybugaboo: LAAAAAAAAMMMMME! Do you want us to come back and pick you up?

goldstandard3000: No, I'm fine. I should spend some more time with my dad. Brenna says that tomorrow is "Ladies Only Day" and we're going to do some girly stuff together. I'm really excited about it.

Jladybugaboo: Really?

goldstandard3000: No, not really.

Why am I spending time with Brenna instead of my dad?

Today my dad had to catch up on some work, so Brenna and I went to the nail salon. I'd never been to one before and it is probably the stinkiest place in the entire universe. All the nail polish smells were making me crazy dizzy.

Don't worry, you'll get used to it.

Then Brenna said, "Pick any color you want!" So I picked blue to match my glasses and then she picked out pink for me.

When we got back to the house, I was going to show my dad my new nails, but Brenna told me that we probably shouldn't bother him while he's working. I didn't see how a visit from the daughter he hasn't seen in **YEARS** would bother him, but I didn't feel like arguing so I helped Brenna make dinner instead.

After dinner we all watched a movie together. Actually, Brenna and I watched a movie while Kyle and Cody played video games and my dad did more work on his laptop.

When the movie was over and Brenna was cleaning up, I asked my dad if we were going to spend any time together, just the two of us.

It would be good to spend a little time with your dad. He really misses you.

Then my dad said

And now it's 3:18 in the
morning and I can't sleep
because I can't believe that I
came all this way to spend
Quality Time with my dad and
he can't even be bothered to take
5 seconds to look at my

STUPID PINK NAILS.

From: goldstandard3000
To: melodylefay

Ohmygodohmygodohmygod I know you're probably not going to get this in time but I think I just did something really stupid but I was upset I'm at Dad and Brenna's and Julie and her dads are in Denver and Brenna wouldn't let me get blue nail polish she made me get pink and Dad won't spend any time with me and I got really mad and I couldn't sleep and then I took some of the Kool-Aid that Brenna uses to make drinks and I mixed it with conditioner and a little water and I smeared it in my hair like you did that one time and then I wrapped my head in one of Brenna's nice pink towels and fell asleep and NOW MY HAIR IS BLUE AND MY HANDS ARE BLUE AND THE TOWEL IS BLUE AND THE PILLOWCASE IS BLUE.

Dad and Brenna are going to wake up ANY SECOND. Dyeing my hair blue seemed like a good idea at 4 am but now it looks like I went crazy and killed a bunch of Smurfs! THEY'RE GOING TO KILL ME. I don't know what I was thinking, I was just tired and mad, what do I do, how do I clean this up???

HELP!!!!!!!!!!

HOW COULD YOU BE SO STUPID?

No television for you, no internet, go to your room, I can't look at you, I'm calling your mother.

Isn't it nice to know that you're raising my daughters to look like huge freaks while you're off gallivanting in Jolly Old England? Great Parenting, Elaine.

Then Brenna came into the guest room with new sheets and told me not to worry about the old ones.

But now I like my hair because if my dad hates it, then it **MUST BE GOOD.** I don't know why I thought it would be a good idea to travel across the country to see him when he can't be bothered to even look at me.

jladybugaboo: Are you online?

jladybugaboo: Are you online?

jladybugaboo: You there?

jladybugaboo: Hellooooooooooooo?

jladybugaboo: Since you're not answering, I can only assume that you're out having a great time. Are you going to be packed up and ready to leave tomorrow? Papa Dad is promising tons of new Fun Facts about Kansas!

jladybugaboo: HALLO CAN YOU READ ME?

jladybugaboo: Are you guys having a power failure or something?

jladybugaboo: Okay, if you don't answer me soon, I'm going to start believing that something is wrong. ARE YOU TRAPPED UNDER SOMETHING HEAVY?

jladybugaboo: I don't know why I'm shout-typing. It's not like using the caps lock button will make you respond any quicker.

jladybugaboo: OR WILL IT?

jladybugaboo: Okay, probably not.

jladybugaboo: Hello?

jladybugaboo: Hello?

I've been up in this room all day long. I slept for a while until Brenna woke me up for dinner. It was pizza, it was too doughy, and Dad wasn't even there.

You look crazy.

She looks like a big blue freak.

You're in so much trouble.

So much trouble!

Boys, knock it off, Lydia's had a rough day.

Rough like her face?

I SAID KNOCK IT OFF.

Now I can't sleep again. It's 5am and Daddy and Papa Dad and Julie are supposed to be picking me up in just five hours!! I can hardly wait.

STUFF I CAN DO IN THE NEXT FIVE HOURS

1. Come up with explanations for why my hair is blue.
2. Glue Kyle and Cody's video games to their butts.
3. Break my dad's computer.
4. Find a way to call my mom.
5. Pack up all my stuff.

I am never coming back here.

EVER.

Our trip to Denver was really neat. We stayed with friends of my dads' from college, and they had a puppy.
Helen
Marci
Anjou!
Normally I don't really like it when dogs lick me, but somehow it's okay if it's a puppy.
Help!
Slobber!

Denver is called "The Mile-High City" because it's a mile above sea level. Helen and Marci kept telling us to drink lots of water to prevent altitude sickness. Daddy and I were pretty good about drinking water, but Papa Dad probably should have had more.

After a while Papa Dad went back to Helen and Marci's house because "Someone needed to look after Anjou."

Roland sent a postcard to me at Helen and Marci's house! I can't believe he remembered.

Hei Julie,
Greetings from Bergen! I am having an excellent time, even though my cousins are making fun of me for turning into an American. They think I'm getting shorter! I think it's because I spend so much time with you.
Adjø, Roland

Julie Graham-Chang
22 Fireweed Ave.
Evergreen, CO 80437
USA

If he's the short one, the rest of his family must be ginormous.

86

The visit was fun, and it was really nice to spend more than one night in the same place, but I was getting worried about Lydia and was happy to get back on the road to pick her up.

Why do you think Lydia hasn't written me back?

Maybe she's been eaten by a rattle snake.

Or kidnapped by cattle thieves.

Nah, she's too skinny. Abducted by aliens?

That's probably it.

DADS!

Relax, sweetie, she was probably too busy.

Too busy being interrogated by our new galactic overlords.

I didn't get to break my dad's computer or glue Kyle and Cody's video games to their butts. I just packed my bag and waited outside for the Graham-Change. My dad said goodbye and left for work, and then Brenna came out and offered me some breakfast.

Don't be angry with your dad. He just doesn't understand that sometimes women like to mix it up and change their looks every once in a while.

I was so happy to see Daddy, Papa Dad, and Julie again.

When we got back on the road, Lydia told us about her visit with Mr. Goldblatt and how her hair turned blue, and then Papa Dad and Daddy took turns making fun of her new hair.

So you wanted to look like the Hindu god of Destruction?

No, she got into a massive brawl with a bunch of Smurfs.

Boring. I already made that joke to Melody.

It was funny, but I couldn't get into it because I was SO MAD at Lydia's stupid dad.

We've stopped for the night in Oakley, Kansas. Lydia took Daddy's cell phone into the bathroom to call her mom. Daddy and Papa Dad have done their best to keep her spirits up, but I can tell that she's pretty upset. I know I am.

Listen sweetie, I know you're really mad at Mr. Goldblatt right now, but I don't think that threatening him with physical violence is going to help Lydia right now. She knows you're her friend, okay?

But he's a jerk and I hate him.

I know, but he's still her father and that's not going to change.

Then I'll hate him quietly.

Okay, sweetie.

STUFF I WOULD HAVE SAID/ DONE to LYDIA'S DAD
(if I'd seen him)

It's probably for the best that you didn't get to see him again.

From: melodylefay
To: goldstandard3000

What happened? Are you okay???? Did Brenna freak out on you? Please write back RIGHT NOW.

From: goldstandard3000
To: melodylefay

Hi Mel,

I'm okay, I'm back with the Graham-Changs and we're in a motel in Kansas. Dad got SO MAD at me. Brenna was actually kind of all right about my hair even though I destroyed a bunch of her linens, but Dad screamed at me and wouldn't let me use the internet and made me stay in the guest room, as if I'd want to hang out with him after the way he acted. He also called Mom and yelled at her and now Mom is super angry with him and told me that I never have to go back to Pueblo if I don't want to. I'm fine, don't worry.

From: melodylefay
To: goldstandard3000

I bet your hair looks awesome. I'm going to write more later, but I have to go right now—these houses aren't building themselves!

Everyone seems to be in a better mood today.

How's our favorite Goldblatt?

I feel a little better.

I don't know, you still look a little blue.

Papa Dad really can't help himself. Today we're going to see the Monument Rocks, which are these weird rock formations that used to be under the sea (about 200,000,000 years ago).

The Monument Rocks, 200 million years ago

The Monument Rocks today

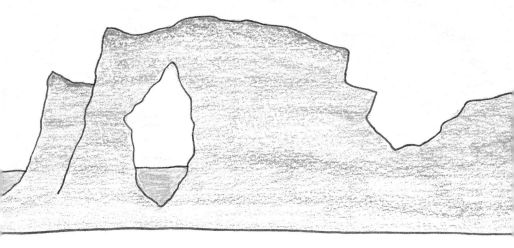

I didn't know that mermaids existed 200 million years ago. I may have taken some artistic liberties. You? Never.

Something we're not quite used to—it's legal to drive 75 miles per hour.

Too fast! Too fast!!!

No worries, we're perfectly legal.

Hey, I know what will calm everyone down—let's sing "Bye Bye Miss American Pie." Ready?

We're also not quite used to hearing that song at least three times a day.

From: melodylefay
To: goldstandard3000

Hey sister,

How's the hair? I bet you're getting some funny looks. Just ignore them. People can be really stupid when you look different.

Things are getting better here. I got a nasty sunburn a while ago but it's kind of turned into a tan. I'm not as dark as Julie, but if I keep working on roofs, I might get there. Izador is still a pain, but he's a pretty good teacher and I know how to use a lot of power tools now. It's pretty fun. There's a guy here named Horatio who pretended to cut off one of his fingers. It was deeply unfunny, and now he's not allowed to use the radial arm saw (which means that I get to use it even more!).

About our father—just forget him. We don't need him, okay?

Melody

Melody wants me to forget about our dad, but I don't know if I can do that. If it weren't for him we wouldn't exist, right? But sometimes I wonder if he's just forgotten about us. Or would like to.

You know you have two dads who totally love you, right?

I know, but they're not technically related to me.

Well, they're not technically related to me, either, when you think about it.

Yeah, but they changed your diapers and stuff.

We've known each other since we were babies. Maybe they did. Should we ask?

Knowing whether or not Daddy and Papa Dad ever changed my diapers is going on my list of **STUFF I NEVER NEED TO KNOW.**

On the road to St. Louis!

My other grandparents, Mah Mah and Yeh Yeh, live in St. Louis, where they moved after they emigrated from China. Daddy was born in St. Louis and his sister, Christina, still lives nearby.

Yeh Yeh

Mah Mah

I haven't seen Mah Mah and Yeh Yeh in a long time but Aunt Christina came over for Thanksgiving a few years ago.

ST. LOUIS!

I assumed we'd be staying with the Changs, but here we are in another hotel. Daddy says it's because their house is too small for all of us to stay over.

It's because they wanted Daddy to marry a woman and they do not approve of Papa Dad and won't have him in their house. They kind of ignore him and have never been to visit us.

How can anyone not like Papa Dad?

What to Wear to a Dinner Out with MAH MAH and YEH YEH

Skirts: We will be Proper Young Ladies.
Long-sleeved shirts: We will be Proper Young Ladies who will melt in the summer heat.
Tank-tops: We will have Improper Arms!
Short-sleeved shirts: We will be slobs.
Short-sleeved shirts we bought in Calico: We will be fake cowgirl slobs.
Shorts: Improper legs! Improper legs!
Pants: We will be HOT. Literally.

Blue hair: I am here to make you look great in comparison.
You're a good friend.

This restaurant better be air-conditioned.

Yes, please.

I'm a little nervous to see Mah Mah and Yeh Yeh — they can be not totally friendly. Every Christmas I get a gift from them but I know that my dads just buy something and say it's from Mah Mah and Yeh Yeh.

Wow, a new watercolor set! Mah Mah and Yeh Yeh always know just what I want!

I think that Daddy and Papa Dad suspect that I'm on to them, but I don't want to let them know because then I probably won't get extra presents, like the time I admitted that I didn't believe in Santa Claus.

And then, just as we were about to leave for dinner...

I had no idea that Papa Dad even had a chin.

It's so weird, I just want to poke him in the face to make sure it's really gone.

Dinner was weird. Yeh Yeh hardly spoke and Mah Mah just asked a lot of questions.

Why you have blue hair?

It was more like being interrogated than an actual conversation. I was so afraid of saying the wrong thing.

And when Mah Mah wasn't asking us questions, she was talking about Daddy's sister.

Christina has a great job. Christina's baby is the best baby, nice and fat. Christina has good husband, he also has good job with promotions. They have vacations in Caribbean.

It was a quiet ride back to the hotel. We were all pretty tired.

Today we're going sightseeing in St. Louis with Papa Dad while Dadd spends the day with Mah Mah and Yeh Yeh. I've been here before but I was super-little, so it doesn't really count. First stop:

The St. Louis Arch
GATEWAY to the WEST!

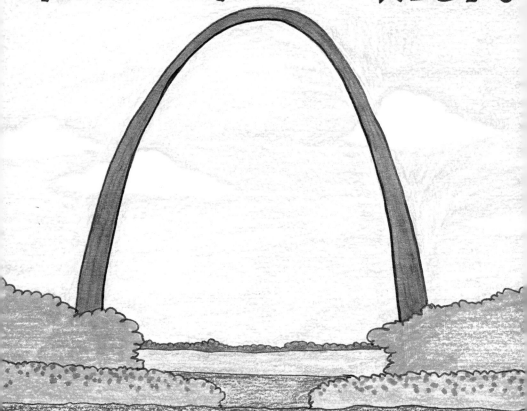

According to the movie that we saw in the St. Louis Arch museum, the St. Louis Arch was constructed in 1963 by many construction men who all had mustaches and weren't afraid of falling to their horrible deaths when they put it together.

According to me, the St. Louis Arch is **HUGE.** We tried to hug it.

YOu tried to hug it.

It seemed friendly.

Did you get enough sleep last night?

Hallo Arch!

I'm going to assume that's a No.

The super-neat thing about the Arch is that you can go inside of it and take an egg-shaped elevator up to the very top, where there are windows.

windows

630ft

The Arch is the tallest National Monument in the United States

You know, these look suspiciously like Fun Facts →

The Arch weighs 17,246 Tons.

AAAHH! I'm turning into Papa Dad!!!

← Egg elevator— only five people can ride in it at a time.

The view from the top of the Arch was **AMAZING**. We could see up and down the Mississippi River, as well as the whole city of St. Louis.

I think I can see Katana from here!

I can see Indiana from here!

I can see into the future from here!

Oooh, what are we having for lunch?

I guess it was a good thing that Daddy wasn't with us. He's not so crazy about heights.

We had a picnic lunch at Forest Park. Papa Dad was kind of quiet, so we tried to cheer him up with our own St. Louis Fun Facts.

Fun Fact! St. Louis was the patron Saint of granola.

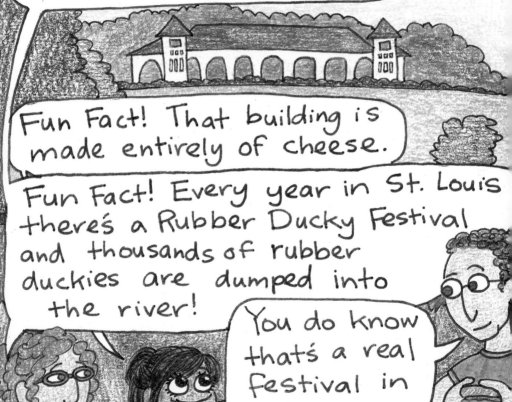

Fun Fact! That building is made entirely of cheese.

Fun Fact! Every year in St. Louis there's a Rubber Ducky Festival and thousands of rubber duckies are dumped into the river!

You do know that's a real festival in Michigan.

You're kidding me.

Tomorrow we're all going to stay with my Aunt Christina.
But tonight Daddy is still at his parents' house. Papa Dad asked us what we wanted for dinner but no one really cared, so we're going to stay at the hotel and order pizza.

You know you're on vacation when you get to eat pizza while sitting on a bed and watching television. I wish Papa Dad was happier.
Yeah.

5:14 am
I can't sleep because I'm still so annoyed with Mah Mah and Yeh Yeh for not inviting us over.

I can't sleep because you're so annoyed. There's nothing we can do about my grandparents. It's just the way they are. What's the point of even having relatives if they don't appreciate you? You're their granddaughter, for goodness' sake! And you get good grades. I want to yell at them.

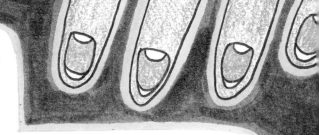

From: goldstandard3000
To: melodylefay

Hi Mel,

Greetings from a hotel room in St. Louis, Missouri! We're here to visit Daddy Chang's family. You'd think that we'd be staying with his parents, but they won't let us. Julie says that it's because they don't like Papa Dad and wish that Daddy would have married a woman instead. It's bumming Papa Dad out and it makes me really, really mad. Why are families so awful? If I ever had a kid and my kid wanted to marry a guy like Papa Dad, I'd be really happy because he's nice and good and I don't think he'd ever divorce Daddy Chang and move thousands of miles away to live with a whole other family and then be a big fat jerk to Julie. People like Papa Dad are hard to find. It's a good thing that we don't have to see them again, because I would probably have to give them a piece of my mind.

Today we're going to visit Julie's aunt in Illinois. Julie says she's cool.

How are you doing? Have you cut off any fingers? If you cut off someone else's fingers, that still counts as a YES. But if you're really good with power tools, Mom told me that she's going to make you fix the roof over the garage.

Love,
Lydia

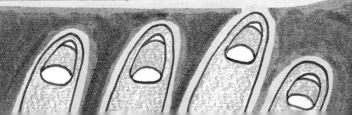

Aunt Christina and her husband, Uncle Donald, live in Collinsville, Illinois, which is about a half-hour east of St. Louis. Collinsville is known as the Horseradish Capital of the World. We don't know what horseradish is, but Papa Dad has promised to let us taste some when we get to Aunt Christina's.

If horseradish is important enough to be the Capital of something, it's got to be good.

Daddy looks tired this morning. Being with his parents stresses him out.

I can relate.

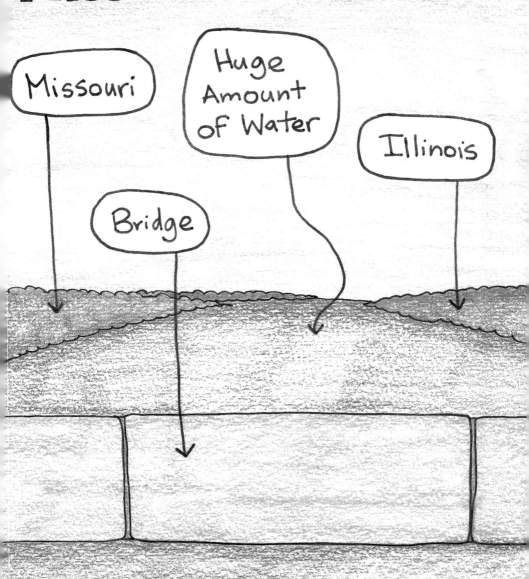

HORSERADISH IS NOT GOOD. NOT GOOD AT ALL.

When will we learn to ignore Papa
Dad when he says, "Taste this!"
There isn't enough water in the
state of Illinois to put out the
fire on my tongue.
I don't think I can feel my mouth
anymore.
Lucky.

Christina and Don have a baby boy named Jason that Mah Mah thinks is "the best baby, nice and fat." I call him Drool Bucket.

He loves you!

You don't have to dislike Jason just because my grandparents like him more than they like me. He's just a baby. It's not his fault.
It is his fault that he produces drool like a running faucet.
I think that's just what babies do.
I believe Jason is above average in drooling. Maybe that's why Mah Mah is so proud. Maybe you should drool more.

I got another postcard from Roland!

I didn't know you got a first postcard from Roland.

He sent it to me in Denver. He's happy to be back in Norway.

What does this one say?

Svidebrua ved Skylstad.
Uraæetra.
Sætremurar på botnen av Lygnstøylsvatnet.
Stavbergsætra.

Hei Julie,
Today we rowed kayaks around the fjords, and then my arms fell off. I am just kidding! I still have arms. The fjords are beautiful. You should come with me to Norway to see them. How is America? ♥ Roland

Nr.: 2049

PRIORITAIRE
PARAVION
A
BL.70.341.12

gen - N-6100 VOLDA
inge@roland.no

Julie Graham-Chang

72 Bethany Ct.

Collinsville, IL 62234

USA

He's such a nice weirdo.

Dinner with Aunt Christina and Uncle Don was fine, except for one sort of awkward moment.

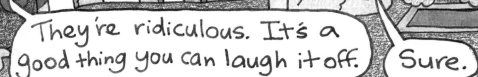

So how were things with Mom and Dad?

Oh, you know. The usual.

They're ridiculous. It's a good thing you can laugh it off.

Sure.

Easy for her to say. Mah Mah and Yeh Yeh don't ignore her husband and they think that Jason poops ice cream. Well, that image is going to be stuck in my head for the next few days. But seriously, why do your dads pretend that everything is okay when it's not?

From: melodylefay
To: goldstandard3000

I bet I could fix the roof over the garage. I could also fix or install a toilet while not cutting off my fingers, and yesterday Izador taught me how to make a window screen. There's this special tool that you use called a spliner, and it looks like a plastic pizza cutter, and you use it to spline the screen. It's pretty cool. I've made about twenty or so screen windows.

I don't know why some families are awful. I just know that when people aren't nice to you, you don't have to be nice to them, so don't even bother. I know you're upset but it's not like you ever have to see Daddy Chang's family again, right? And Julie's okay, so forget about them. Life is too short to deal with mean people.

Did I tell you that Izador put me in charge of a team? It's not a huge team (there are only four of us) but we're responsible for installing twelve toilets. I'm calling us Team Potty Party. What do you think?

Say hi to Julie and the dads,
Melody

We should make this into a tee shirt for Melody when we get home

It was nice to see Aunt Christina, but we were all kind of happy to get back on the road. On the way out of town Papa Dad made us stop by The World's Largest Catsup Bottle.

It's actually a water tower that's been made to look like a bottle of catsup.

Or ketchup.
We wondered if it could actually be called the World's Largest Bottle of Catsup (or Ketchup) if there was no catsup (or ketchup) inside.

The GREAT CATSUP BOTTLE DEBATE!
But it's not a real ketchup bottle!
It would be, if it were filled with ketchup.
But it's not. It's full of water.
What if I took a regular ketchup bottle, poured the ketchup out, and filled it with water. Would it still be a ketchup bottle?
Why would you do that?
Yes, because it once contained ketchup.
How do you know that the water tower was never full of ketchup?
This lasted AN HOUR.

After driving east for a while, Papa Dad made us stop at a town called Vandalia to see a dragon. How on earth does he know about these things?

There's a store near the dragon that sells tokens, and if you put the token in the dragon, IT WILL BREATHE FIRE.

I think Papa Dad's gone crazy.

Should you be driving?

TO THE DRAGON!

We spent about twelve dollars making the dragon breathe fire again and again and again.

SO COOL. I'm going to tell my mom that we need one for our yard.

We got back on the road and headed for Indianapolis. On the way, the weirdest thing happened.

I can't believe that we actually know most of the lyrics to that song now. So weird.
Weirder than a blue-haired girl putting tokens into a fire-breathing dragon?
Maybe.

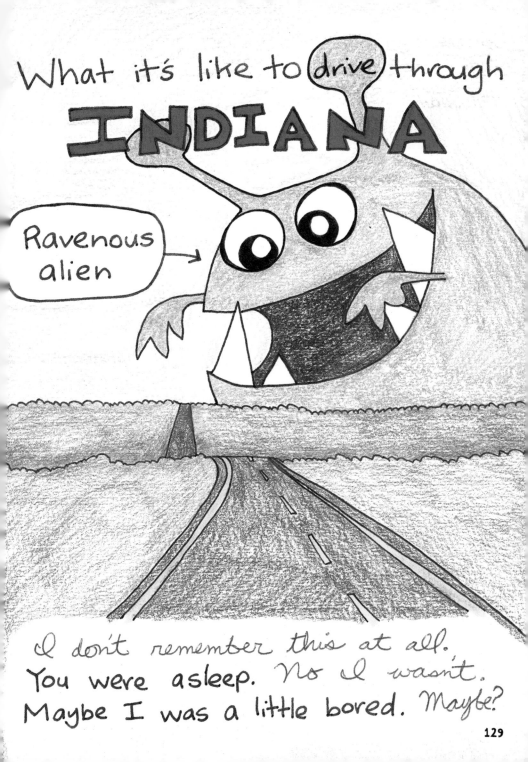

INDIANAPOLIS!

Indianapolis is called Circle City, mostly because of the enormous Soldiers' and Sailors' Monument that's in a big circle in the middle of the city.

We drove around the monument about seven times until Daddy pointed out that we were just wasting gas, and then we parked and walked around it instead.

We're going to be here for two nights before we go to Ohio to visit with Papa Dad's sister Kat and her family to stay with them and drop off most of the stuff that we've been hauling from Nana and Grandpa Jim's old house.

It seems like a million billion years since we were in California.

OUR JOURNEY
(so far)

America is so much bigger than I thought it would be.

Today we went to the Indianapolis Children's Museum. We tried to explain to the dads that we're clearly too old to go to a children's museum, but they insisted that we at least go to see the outside of the building. COOLEST OUTSIDE OF A MUSEUM EVER.

But do you breathe fire?

You don't scare me.

There were life-sized dinosaurs bursting out of and crawling all over the museum. So awesome.

It was such a nice day that no one minded just sitting and letting me take the time to draw the dinosaurs (except maybe Papa Dad, who took the time to become an art critic).

That dinosaur needs purple wings.

I'm drawing what I see, not what goofy thing you think I should see.

Draw us riding a dinosaur!

I'm ignoring you.

While Julie was drawing the dinosaurs, Daddy Chang sat down with me and asked if I felt like giving my dad a call.

Melody says I should just forget about him.

Do you want to forget about him?

I don't know. He's pretty much forgotten about us.

I don't believe he's forgotten about you. Both you and your sister are pretty unforgettable.

What's the point of talking to him? He doesn't know who I am and he hasn't bothered to find out.

But if you never talk to him again, he'll never have the opportunity to learn who you are, and you'll never get to know him.

I almost couldn't believe what I said next.

But you've been talking to your parents for a million billion years and they still don't accept who you are, and they make everyone miserable. Why should I be miserable?

Daddy Chang looked shocked and sort of sad and I really wanted to take back everything that I'd said and shove it back into my big dumb mouth, but it was too late. I thought he was going to

I am an adult and my parents are none of your business, you blue-haired weirdo!

Find your own way home!!!

Of course he didn't actually say that.

I've always known that my parents weren't able to really accept me, or James, or even Julie. You've seen that.

So why do you bother with them?

Because even if they never can be the parents I want them to be, I can be the person that I want to be. I try to love them for who they are and give them a chance.

But what about the way they treat Julie and Papa Dad?

And then Daddy said

That's why we don't see them very often, but we do keep them in our lives.

So you think I should call my dad?

Do you think your sister is happy pretending he doesn't exist?

Melody's never happy.

I think you should do what makes you happy. When you're ready.

I swear, if you ever stop talking to your dads, I'll totally stop talking to you.
What did I do?

So do you think you'll call your dad?

Maybe. But what would I say?

What do you usually talk about when he calls you?

School is good. My teachers are okay. I'm in the school musical... My grades are pretty good.

Maybe we can make you some cue cards or something.

THINGS LYDIA COULD TALK ABOUT WITH HER DAD

So Lydia's decided to wait a while to call her dad.

If I call him at all.

If she calls him at all.

From: goldstandard3000
To: melodylefay

Team Potty Party sounds kind of gross but also kind of cool, so I say go for it. When I told Julie, she drew a picture of a toilet with a party hat on—remind me to show it to you when we get home.

I talked over some stuff with Daddy Chang and I think I might give Dad a call. I don't know. I'm kind of mad at him but he is our dad, right? I know you don't want to talk to him, but would you be mad if I did?

We're about to head off to White River State Park to watch some people fly kites. I know, it sounds kind of lame, but so far most of the stuff that Papa Dad comes up for us to see is kind of awesome. Remind me to tell you about the dragon when we get home…

Do you think Melody's going to be mad?

Well, she's kind of always mad. *True.*

Daddy bought a kite for us to fly, but we just watched as he and Papa Dad tried to get it to work.

I thought you said you knew how to do this.

I've seen it done before.

I've seen astronauts in space before, but that doesn't mean I know how to be an astronaut.

Tomorrow we go to see Aunt Kat in Ohio!

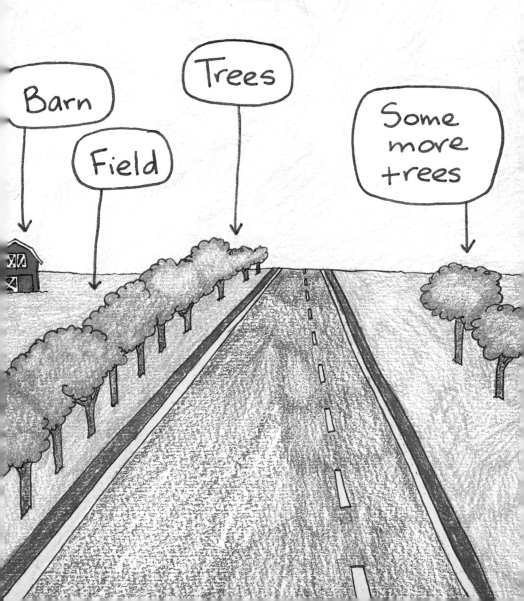

We've decided to go straight to Oberlin instead of staying overnight in Columbus, even though Columbus is the Capital of Ohio and therefore full of Fun Facts. Everyone is pretty tired of always being in the car and staying in hotels.

I never thought I'd get sick of hotels, because it's always so great to have your bed made for you.

We won't miss the little hotel shampoo and conditioner bottles.

Because we've collected about ten bajillion of them.

We'd been driving for a while when we began to see these signs—

and we all wondered if it was a barn that stored cheese, or a barn made entirely out of cheese.

That couldn't not be stinky.

The barn was totally not made out of cheese, but we did stop there for lunch.

Aunt Kat is Papa Dad's sister. She's married to Uncle Nate and they have three kids.

Aunt Kat

Murphy
(49, in doggie years)

Uncle Nate

Jake (17)

Sara (13)

Molly (5)

We usually spend a week with them every summer, and sometimes they come to our house on Thanksgiving. They're great, even if Uncle Nate tells the Same Ancient Joke every time we see him.

The Graham-Mackesseys are so huggy!

Hello my little cookie monster!

Hi Aunt Kat.

Yeah, everyone on Papa Dad's side of the family is super-huggy. You get used to it. Murphy has.

My doggie is the best doggie in the whole world!

Not so tight, Molly.

Okay!

Papa Dad and Daddy get to stay in the guestroom and we're getting an air mattress in my cousin Sara's room. She shares a bathroom with my cousin Jake, which is gross since boys stink up bathrooms.

Take some bandanas — I use them to cover my face if I need to go to the bathroom right after my brother has used it.

We understand. We totally broke into the Boys' Bathroom at school a few months ago.

Cool.

Tonight we're having a family dinner with everyone except for Jake, who has some sort of band rehearsal, and tomorrow we're going to help Aunt Kat and Uncle Nate unpack the trailer.

Another postcard from Roland! Aunt
Kat gave it to me after dinner.

Kjenndalsbreen - Loen - Nordfjord
Juli 1996
Foto: Ø. Søbye/Samfoto

Hei Julie,

By my calculations,
you have now been
in 9 different states!
That is crazy! I can't
wait to see you and
hear all about your
crazy trip.
♥ Roland
p.s. say hei to Lydia

Julie Graham-Chang
14 Cedar Lane
Oberlin, OH 44074
USA

Nr. 6878/6

Printed in Norway

3 postcards sent to 3 different places?
Roland is so in love with you.
He's European. Maybe Europeans just
love sending postcards.
If that were true, he'd be sending
some to me as well, but no, he just
sends them to you.
He said hi to you! I feel super-special.

Unpacking the trailer was weird. But it seems like so long ago since we packed it up in California. But Kat was pretty excited to get Nana and Grandpa Jim's old stuff.

Oh my gosh, look, Sara, my old dollhouse!

Mom, I'm thirteen.

Oh my gosh, look, Molly, my old dollhouse!

Hooray!

Things that are seriously cool about your cousin Jake.

1. Jake is in a rock band.
2. Jake drives his own car.
3. Jake is really mature.
4. Jake knows whats cool and whats lame.

How is that possibly true? He thinks the worlds scariest bird made out of knotted ropes is cool.

It is cool! Jake understands. It's so ugly, it's cool.

I can't wait to see you explain that to everyone at school.

Oh, this old thing? I picked it up in California.

It's official. Lydia is totally in love with my cousin Jake.

I am not! But did you hear him say my hair is cool?

Sara says this happens every time one of her friends comes over, so she's stopped inviting her friends to the house when she knows that Jake is going to be around.

That's ridiculous. I don't like him, I just respect his opinions and stuff.

It's going to be a long week.

What it's like to be around **Lydia** when **Lydia** is around **Jake**

① Everything Jake does is SO COOL.

So... whatcha doing?

Loading the dishwasher.

Cool.

② Everything Jake says is IMPORTANT.

Has anyone seen the nail clippers?

Accidentally scratching someone would be bad.

③ Everything Jake thinks is AMAZING.

Maybe I'll shave my head.

That would be amazing.

Oh shut up.

Aunt Kat works as a professor at the nearby college, so she never has to work during the summer.

So you totally don't have to go in to work?

No, but summer is when I do all of my research.

We do research all the time. It's not really work.
Seriously. We should become professors.

Let's research burritos.

Brilliant idea! It should take us 3 or so months.

Let's get to work!

Things your Parents Neglect to Tell you in Advance

(even though you've spent eighty quadrillion hours in the car with them)

We're going CAMPING!

YAY!

This could be really exciting!

What Lydia doesn't understand about going camping with Aunt Kat and Uncle Nate: When they camp, they really aren't kidding.

~~How bad could it be?~~

What Lydia Thinks Camping is Like

Sleeping on the ground is great! I feel awesome and I have no need to go to the bathroom!

Hey Lydia, I found these wild unicorns! Want to go for a ride with me? There's a rainbow that we can take to a super-cool cloud-land where we can kiss!

Hey.

I'm mythical!

Wow, unicorns? Is that what I think camping is like?
Hey, they're your super-magical thoughts. I'm just recording them.

When Daddy, Papa Dad, and I go camping, that means we rent out a cabin in the woods that's near a whole lot of other cabins and a short walk to a bathroom.

When Kat and Nate go camping, that means we walk through the woods for one hundred hours with all our gear to the middle of nowhere and bury our own poop.

Stop being so negative. We'll have fun.

We have reached our campground!
Finally. It's near a creek.

After we found our campsite it was our job to gather dry wood for the campfire. It was pretty easy.

I was so happy not to have a huge, heavy pack on my back any more. But Sara acted like looking for firewood was the worst chore in the world.

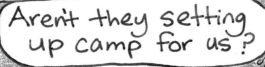

I can't believe that we have to do this. What are they doing? Nothing. It's so unfair.

Aren't they setting up camp for us?

Sure, so they can sit around doing nothing in their tents.

I thought they were making us dinner.

She's a little cranky. She'll get over it.

When we got back to camp, everything was set up and Uncle Nate had started the campfire. Papa Dad got kind of ambitious with dinner.

Eating around a campfire is great.
Cleaning up afterward really makes me appreciate dishwashers.

Your uncle is ridiculous.

Papa Dad wanted to tell ghost stories after dinner, but everyone was pretty pooped out and wanted to go to sleep. He seemed disappointed, so we let him tell one if he promised it would take less than a minute.

It was a moonless night in these very woods, and there was a family on a camping trip (who happened to set up camp RIGHT HERE). They were having a good time, even though one had worked really hard on a totally unappreciated summer vegetable ratatouille...

Everyone in the family wen
to sleep, except for the
oldest daughter, Clara.
Seriously, Uncle Jimmy?
Shh. Clara was hungry... strangely hungry for summer vegetable ratatouille, so she slippe out of her tent to get some from the bear bag...
All our food goes in a bear bag, which is hung from a tree so bears can't get it.
You're kidding me.

 But when she reached the bag, Clara saw, to her great Horror—

That someone had already eaten the ratatouille!

That someone hadn't eaten the ratatouille?

That there was a human head inside the bear bag?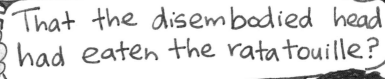

 That the disembodied head had eaten the ratatouille?

 WHOSE HEAD WAS IN THE BAG?

Maybe it's time to call it a night.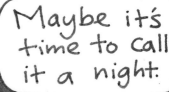

I don't know if I got enough sleep to be an expert on what it's like to sleep in a tent.

DAWN at the CAMPSITE
Good morning ladies! How did you sleep?
Bluh.
Duh.
I have to go to the bathroom.
Here you go!
You're kidding.

HOW TO POOP IN THE WOODS

1. Find a private place that's at least 200 feet from any water source.

2. Dig a "cat hole."

3. Do your business in the cat hole.

8"

This takes some aiming skills.

4. Bury your business and a very small amount of used toilet paper in the cat hole. 5. RUN AWAY!

We've just been informed that we're going to hike to the nearby lake to go fishing so that we have something to eat for dinner.

Have you done this before?

Sort of.

Oh my god, Jake saved your life? Perhaps it was unwise to tell you that story.

JUST IN CASE I HAPPEN to ALMOST DROWN TODAY

On the off-chance that I just happen to fall out of the boat while we're fishing, someone should probably call for Jake to help out because he clearly has experience with that sort of thing.

I saved you!

Thanks!

Actually, Aunt Kat was a registered lifeguard, so she's probably the better bet. Remind me not to get in the same boat as Kat.

Also, you know how to swim.

I'm really tired! I could forget how.

There are rowboats at the lake that anyone can use, so after an exciting breakfast of dry cereal, we all hiked down to the water. Your uncle kept pointing out which plants could be eaten, but it seemed like he was just making stuff up.

That's edible, and those are edible, and we should pick some of those later for a nice salad...

The leftover ratatouille is beginning to sound better and better.

So I didn't almost drown today, which is probably a good thing, seeing how almost drowning in 3½ feet of water would make me look absurd.

Help me.
Save me.
I can't swim.

Seriously?

I did, however, impress everyone with my superior fishing skills.

HOW to CLEAN a FISH

1. Scrape off the scales

2. Slit the belly.

3. Scrape out the guts.

4. Seriously consider becoming a vegetarian.

I don't know if I'm hungry any more.

Weird side-of-the-trail salad is looking pretty good right now.

Our Menu for Tonight

Appetizer
CRACKERS WITH SUMMER
VEGETABLE RATATOUILLE

Second Course
SALAD OF WILD GREENS
WITH CHERRY TOMATOES THAT
SEEM TO APPEAR, SUSPICIOUSLY,
OUT OF THE BEAR BAG

Main Course
FIRE-ROASTED FISH OF SOME
SORT THAT WE MAY OR
MAY NOT TRY

Alternate Main Course
PEANUT BUTTER SANDWICH

Dessert
FRESH-PICKED
BLACK BERRIES

I hate to admit it, but your Uncle Nate was right — it is super-satisfying to eat a fish that you caught yourself.

I don't think we ate the fish we caught. I think we ate the fish he caught. I'm pretty sure he threw our fish back in the lake.

I choose to believe we were eating the fish I caught, which was, for the record, enormous.

Riiiiiight.

After dinner Jake took out his
guitar and played some songs for us.
If Jake lived in my house with
his guitar, I'd never watch teevee.
I bet you wouldn't. Jake had been
playing for a while when all of a
sudden the music got familiar.

I could kiss the dads for making
us learn that song! Jake was crazy
impressed that I knew all the words.

After the singing we were all pretty wiped out, so we went to our tents without hearing the rest of Papa Dad's ghost story.

I don't think there is a rest of Papa Dad's story. I suspect he was making it up as he went along.

That's entirely possible.

He was probably going to finish the story by having us all eaten by a bear.

That had been hiding in the bear bag all along.

We put our hands over your
mouth so you wouldn't scream!

I had never heard a bear before, but Sara had, so she woke me up by putting her hand over my mouth.

Don't freak out, but I think there's a bear outside.

mmrph!

At first I thought she was kidding, but then I clearly heard a bear. Either a bear or a five-hundred pound human being crashing around the campsite.

I wasn't scared. Yes you were. I wasn't scared until I remembered that Jake was sleeping outside.

WHAT TO DO WHEN A
BEAR IS NEAR

1. Stay very, very still.
2. Stay very, very quiet.
3. Try not to cry.
4. Try to stay calm when you hear the bear getting closer and closer and closer to your tent.

5. Do not hit the bear with a dinky plastic flashlight.

I wasn't going to attack it! I was just preparing to protect us!
The bear must have been right outside of the front of our tent...

189

Because there's no way it could have gotten so much pee on the tent if it had been further away.

After the bear was done soaking our tent, we heard it wander off and stayed as still as possible until Papa Dad poked his head into our tent.

And how are we all doing at this lovely hour? Your tent feels oddly wet.

What Happened Outside Our Tent
(while we weren't moving or making a sound)

He slept through the whole thing!
How cool is that ???

Once we realized that no one had been eaten by a bear, we all decided to pack up our things and head back to the cars.

> If we don't pack up camp and go home right now, I'm going to scream until the bear comes back to eat us all.

Sara can be a little...dramatic, but I don't think anyone (besides maybe Uncle Nate) really wanted to keep camping especially in our tent. So we packed everything up and started to hike back by the time the sun came up.

We're back at Aunt Kat and Uncle Nate's house. I ♥ indoor plumbing.

From: melodylefay
To: goldstandard3000

I won't be mad at you if you decide to call our biological paternal parental unit but I just don't understand why you feel like you need to talk to him again. What good could come of it? Has he ever acted the way that you'd want a dad to act?

Whatever you choose to do, don't worry about me being mad. I'm totally beyond that.

In other news—today we finished an entire housing unit! It's so great, I'll can't wait to show you and Mom the pictures when I get home. Where in the country are you now?

So are you going to call your dad?
Maybe. But more importantly, how excited are we to see Jake rehearse with his band tonight?

I've got band rehearsal tonight— you guys want to come and jam?

I LIKE TO JAM!

Oh for pity's sake.

I don't know if I should encourage it, but I am kind of excited. I've never heard Jake's band before—it'll be a neat way to spend our second-to-last night in Ohio.

I can't believe we have to leave. So lame.

Jake's band is called **CARCASS**.

I can't tell why Giggling Girl is there — Awesome Girl is taking care of the percussion just fine.

I think she's Jake's girlfriend.

Her rhythm is _nonexistent._

Despite Giggling Girls rhythm issues that she didn't have any Carcass didn't sound that bad.
They sounded **AMAZING**. Especially after Jake asked if I wanted to jam with them.

Hey Blue, want to jump in?

I just made up some background harmonies as we went along, and it was **FANTASTIC**.
I couldn't tell what the songs were about. Could you?
Did it even matter? I was part of a real band!

When we got home I felt kind of ready to call my dad. I didn't really know what I was going to say, but I felt like it was better to say anything than to stay quiet. Like Jake said

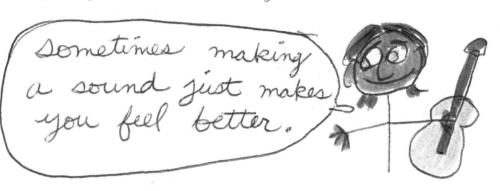

Sometimes making a sound just makes you feel better.

So I called my dad. What did he say?

Hi Dad, we're in Ohio... the weather is good. We went camping with Julie's cousins... it was good... we'll be going home tomorrow.

Not much.

Are you okay?
Yeah. I know who my real family is.

From: melodylefay
To: goldstandard3000

Also, remember that whatever happens, you'll always have a sister who loves you and can install a toilet.

In just an hour we'll be back in our home state!

It's almost like we never left and drove over three thousand miles!

I believe Papa Dad intends to sing "American Pie" over and over for the last two hundred miles.

In spite of that, I think I might actually miss seeing Daddy and Papa Dad every day.

Do you think you'll miss your dad, too?

Maybe a little. But I'll always have Melody and Mom.

And you know you can always come over whenever you want to hear Papa Dad sing.

I know.

jladybugaboo: It's so weird to be home! Everything looks different but kind of the same at the same time. Is it weird for you?

goldstandard3000: You would not believe—you have to come over tomorrow to see Melody. She's a little different...

Acknowledgments

Thank you, thank you, thank you to the fantastic Amulet staff, whose dedication to bringing my books to readers has been an author's dream: Susan Van Metre, Scott Auerbach, Melissa Arnst, Chris Blank, Chad Beckerman, Maria Middleton, Laura Mihalick, Mary Ann Zissimos, and the indefatigable Jason Wells. Crazy heaps of lovin' thanks go to Maggie Lehrman, the editor with the mostest, who understands and supports my occasional need to invent words. Thanks are also due to Marie Elcin and her art students, for providing me with terrific photographs, and Jim Cason, for introducing me to Eline Oftedal and Arve Larsen; Tusen takk to them for sending blank postcards from Norway to a complete stranger. Many thanks as well to Kit Burke-Smith and Nate Smith, for the camping stories—your ability to not get eaten by bears was inspirational.

As always, many thanks go to Stephen Barr and all the wonderful people at Writers House, especially my stupendous agent, Dan Lazar, who believed in Lydia and Julie back when they were mere glints of an idea. Sincere thank-yous go out to all the friends and family members who have encouraged me to continue to write and illustrate, and then encouraged everyone they know to read what I've written and illustrated. Thanks to all the booksellers I've met across the country who have welcomed me into their shops and introduced me to their cities, and to all the wonderful readers who have made continuing Lydia and Julie's adventures possible.

Finally, I give my love and gratitude to my best friend and partner, Mark.

About the Author

Amy Ignatow is a cartoonist and the author of THE POPULARITY PAPERS series. She is a graduate of Moore College of Art and Design and also makes a decent tureen of chicken soup. Amy lives in Philadelphia with her husband, Mark, their daughter, Anya, and their cat, Mathilda, who just isn't very bright.

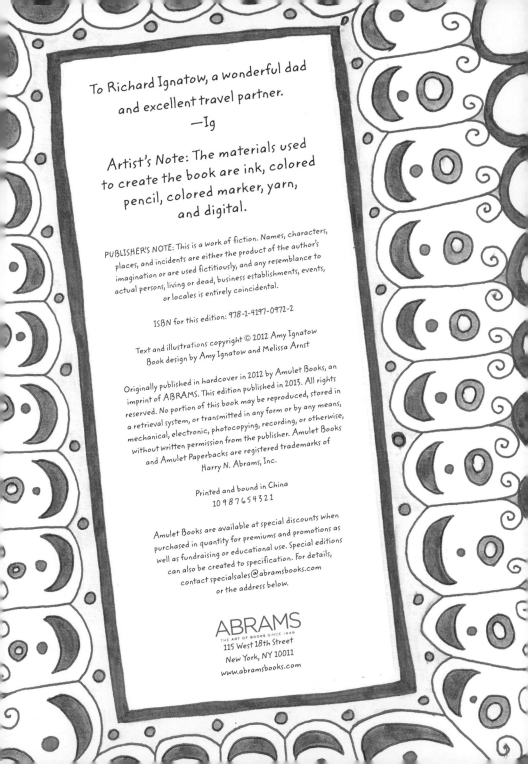

To Richard Ignatow, a wonderful dad
and excellent travel partner.
—Ig

Artist's Note: The materials used
to create the book are ink, colored
pencil, colored marker, yarn,
and digital.

ISBN for this edition: 978-1-4197-0972-2

Text and illustrations copyright © 2012 Amy Ignatow
Book design by Amy Ignatow and Melissa Arnst

Originally published in hardcover in 2012 by Amulet Books, an imprint of ABRAMS. This edition published in 2013. All rights reserved. No portion of this book may be reproduced, stored in a retrieval system, or transmitted in any form or by any means, mechanical, electronic, photocopying, recording, or otherwise, without written permission from the publisher. Amulet Books and Amulet Paperbacks are registered trademarks of Harry N. Abrams, Inc.

Printed and bound in China
10 9 8 7 6 5 4 3 2 1

Amulet Books are available at special discounts when purchased in quantity for premiums and promotions as well as fundraising or educational use. Special editions can also be created to specification. For details, contact specialsales@abramsbooks.com or the address below.

ABRAMS
THE ART OF BOOKS SINCE 1949
115 West 18th Street
New York, NY 10011
www.abramsbooks.com

Catch up with all of The Popularity Papers

Book One: Research for the Social Improvement and General Betterment of Lydia Goldblatt & Julie Graham-Chang
by Amy Ignatow

Hardcover
ISBN 978-0-8109-8421-9 · U.S. $15.95 Can. $19.95 U.K. £9.99

Paperback
ISBN 978-0-8109-9723-3 · U.S. $8.95 Can. $9.95 U.K. £5.99

Book Two: The Long-Distance Dispatch Between
Lydia Goldblatt & Julie Graham-Chang
by Amy Ignatow

Hardcover
ISBN 978-0-8109-9724-0 · U.S. $15.95 Can. $18.95 U.K. £9.99

Paperback
ISBN 978-1-4197-0183-2 · U.S. $8.95 Can. $9.95 U.K. £5.99

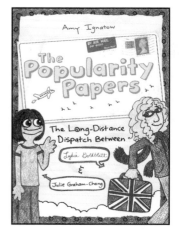

Book Three: Words of (Questionable) Wisdom
from Lydia Goldblatt & Julie Graham-Chang
by Amy Ignatow

Hardcover
ISBN 978-1-4197-0063-7 · U.S. $15.95 Can. $17.95 U.K. £9.99